KAI: NINJA OF FIRE

By Greg Farshtey

SCHOLASTIC INC.

New York   Toronto   London   Auckland
Sydney   Mexico City   New Delhi   Hong Kong

ISBN 978-0-545-34827-0

LEGO, the LEGO logo, the Brick and Knob configurations and the Minifigure are trademark of the LEGO Group. © 2011 The LEGO Group. Produced by Scholastic Inc. under license from the LEGO Group.
Published by Scholastic Inc. SCHOLASTIC and associated logos are trademarks and/or registered trademarks of Scholastic Inc.

20 19 18   15 16/0

Printed in the U.S.A.   40
First printing, August 2011

CONTENTS

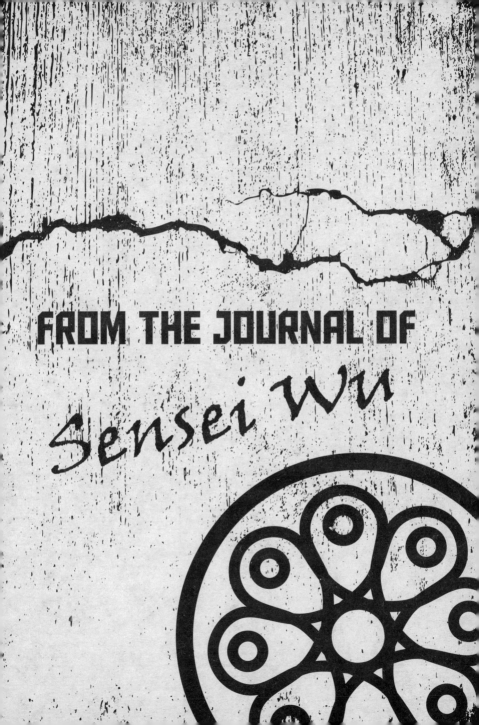

FROM THE JOURNAL OF

Sensei Wu

f the four young men I recruited to join my fight against Garmadon, easily the most . . . challenging was Kai. He was the last of the group and my hope was that he would become the Ninja of Fire. Certainly his temperament made him ideal for that element.

Kai is the son of one of my oldest and most trusted friends. He and his sister, Nya, were raised by their father. They lived in a little village, far from any major city, a place where one could work and strive for years and never be known outside the small

settlement. Kai's father worked as a black-smith and his apprentice was Kai.

Training Kai in the art of forging weapons and armor was, I gather, not an easy task, for the same reason it has not been easy to train him to be a ninja. He is impatient, reck-less, quick to anger, and reluctant to listen to the advice of others. His manner can be brash, but I believe that is a shield he has built against the world. With the passing of his father, Kai became the man of the family with the responsibility to look after his sister. That can be a great burden for a youth.

I found Kai and Nya at work in their shop, 4 Weapons. Unfortunately, Samukai and his skeleton warriors arrived at the same time, in search of a map that marked the locations of the Four Weapons of Spinjitzu. The skeletons attacked, and in the battle, made off with both the map and Nya. I convinced Kai that by accepting my training, he would have

the best chance to retrieve his sister safely.

With the help of my other three young warriors, I set about teaching him what I could about the art of battle. It was not easy. The challenge was how to break him of his bad habits — rash actions, dangerous risk taking, and letting his emotions cloud his thoughts — without breaking his spirit. The other three, Cole, Jay, and Zane, had had more time together and knew how to work as a team. Kai was used to being on his own, except for Nya, and was reluctant to rely on others.

Ah, Nya . . . I do not know why Garmadon ordered the young girl's capture, except perhaps to use as a hostage against me in the future. Its most immediate effect was on Kai. He was consumed with the desire to rescue her, which blinded him to almost everything else. I feared that in the heat of battle he would put himself or the others in danger out of concern for Nya.

Still, there was much potential in Kai—potential that I am happy to say was realized. He is brave, loyal, intelligent, and willing to work hard to better himself. He has speed and grace, two key ingredients in mastering Spinjitzu. He is also fearless. I have no doubt he would challenge Garmadon himself in single combat if given half a chance, and never feel a moment's hesitation.

I look at Kai and I see his father. They share the same tendency to rush headlong into danger, the same passion for life and devotion to family, and even some of Kai's moves in mock combat echo his father's. Kai did not know of his father's past, thinking of him only as a simple blacksmith, until I told him.

In the end, I am happy to say that Kai justified my faith in him. He earned the Sword of Fire he wields now. More important, he learned to work as part of a team and to see the grand picture of the world rather than

focusing on just his corner of it. He could have left with Nya and returned to his village and his old life, and no one would have thought less of him for it. But he chose to stand beside his partners and prepare for any future danger that might threaten.

Does he still leap into danger?

Yes. Is he still both amazing and exasperating? Yes. Is he like the fire he wields, burning hot and bright no matter what? Yes, indeed. He is Kai, unique as a spark of flame, sharp as the sword he carries, a true hero at last.

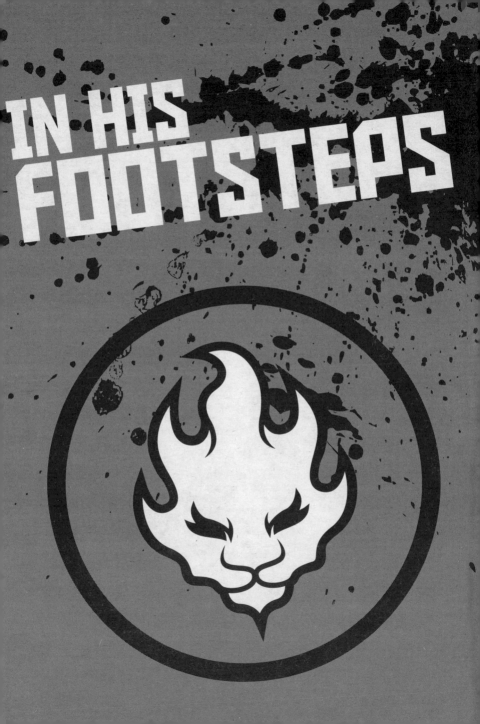

Kai crouched down, his brow knitted in concentration. His eyes were locked on the practice dummy ten feet away. It was just a thing of cloth and sticks, but it seemed to be making fun of him. He could almost hear it saying, "Ha! You call that a flying kick? You look like a chicken trying to fly . . . with one wing . . . blindfolded."

The young would-be ninja broke into a run. On his fifth stride, he planted his right foot and leaped into the air. His left foot was pointed straight out before him and aimed right at the target dummy's head. This time,

Kai would knock the head off. He was sure of it.

Just short of contact, he faltered. His left leg dropped perhaps half an inch, just enough to throw off his balance. He fought to correct it, but that only made the problem worse. Suddenly, his flying kick had turned into a confused jumble, arms and legs going every which way. Kai landed on his rear end, bounced, rolled, and wound up at the foot of the practice dummy.

Nearby, Sensei Wu looked on. After a moment, he began to slowly **clap his hands**. "Amazing," he said. "Not just anyone can botch a flying kick that badly. That takes real talent."

Kai got to his feet, brushing the dirt off his clothes. That had been his twelfth attempt at the maneuver, and his twelfth failure. He was angry at himself. His sister, Nya, was missing, captured by skeleton warriors, and she needed him to save her. And here he was struggling to master the battle techniques he would need to know, while time was running out.

For the first time, he began to doubt. What if Sensei Wu had been wrong to choose him for training? What if he didn't have what it took to be a ninja, or to learn the art of Spinjitzu? Maybe he was just a blacksmith, as his father had been. Was he fooling himself that he could ever become a warrior?

"Try it again," repeated Sensei Wu, sipping from his cup of tea. Kai had never seen him actually make any tea, but he always seemed to have a cup of it on hand.

"What's the use?" Kai answered, his eyes on the ground. "Maybe I'm not cut out for this. Maybe I should go back to making swords and armor."

Sensei Wu smiled, remembering the incredibly bad sword he had seen Kai forge. "Yes, as I recall, you were a master at that."

Kai shot him a hard look. "Okay, so maybe

my work was a little . . . creative. At least I knew which end of the sword to put in the fire. Here? I'm not a ninja. I work in a blacksmith shop in a market square, just like my father did. I've lived in that village my whole life, the same as he did. We're just regular people. We're not **warriors and adventurers**."

Sensei Wu gently eased himself down onto a chair. He was looking in Kai's direction, but his eyes were focused on a past time. When he spoke, it was very quietly.

"Your father," Sensei Wu said, "did not live in that village all his life."

"What are you talking about?" asked Kai. "You told me that when you decided to hide the Four Weapons of Spinjitzu from your evil brother, you came to our village. You asked my father to draw a map showing the locations of the four hiding places."

"True," said Sensei Wu. "And from that day to this, I had never set foot in your village again . . . because your father asked me not to."

Kai looked at the sensei in disbelief. "That's crazy. You're a sensei, a master of Spinjitzu, and you let a blacksmith tell you where you could and couldn't go?"

"No," Sensei Wu answered. "I respected the wishes of my best friend."

Seeing the expression on Kai's face, Sensei Wu smiled softly. "You look surprised. Did you not think Spinjitzu masters had friends? There was a time when your father and I traveled the length of this land, righting wrongs and aiding the weak. That was long before you were born, of course, or your sister."

"Are you saying my father knew **Spinjitzu**?"

Sensei Wu shook his head. "No. He could have, if he had chosen that path. But he did not."

There was an uncomfortable silence.

Finally, Kai sat down at Sensei Wu's feet and said, "I never knew any of this. Tell me about him . . . please."

"Your father was wise, brave, and the most trusted ally any man could have," Sensei Wu began. "We fought together for many years, sometimes even with Garmadon beside us, before my brother turned bad. We brought peace where there had been disorder. Your father was a hero, Kai."

The sensei smiled. "In the early days, he was much like you—headstrong, reckless. Once, we were searching for a group of samurai bandits. Your father was sure he saw them in a nearby field in the moonlight. Without waiting for me, he drew his sword and **charged**."

"What happened?" asked Kai.

"In the morning, we had to pay the farmer for all the scarecrows your father had 'defeated,'" the sensei said with a chuckle.

"As time passed, Garmadon and I grew

further apart. I came to rely on your father's advice and aid more and more. Yet another life beckoned to him. He had met and married the woman who would be your mother. Eventually, you and Nya were born. He chose to lay down his sword, settle in that village, and be with his family."

"Why?" asked Kai. "Why would he choose to live in a little out-of-the-way place when he had a life full of adventure?"

"I asked the same question, at the time," answered Sensei Wu. "Your father's answer was, 'Protecting the world begins with protecting the ones you love. There are many men who can wield a sword or win a battle. But only I can be a husband to my wife and a father to Kai and Nya.'"

Kai shrugged. It still didn't make sense to him. "And that was it? You two said good-bye?"

Sensei Wu nodded. "For a very long time, yes—where I traveled, danger traveled with

me, and your father did not want his children put in jeopardy. When I finally defeated Garmadon and chose to hide the Weapons of Spinjitzu, I knew I had to share the secret of their location with someone I trusted."

"So you came to my father," said Kai.

"He made the map and hid it where we hoped no one would find it—inside the banner of your shop," Sensei Wu replied. "He knew it was a risk, keeping it there, but it was a greater one to allow it out of his sight. And I slept peacefully, knowing it was in his care."

"But Garmadon found it anyway."

Sensei Wu nodded. Kai said nothing for a long time. Finally, he looked up and asked, "Do you think my father would be proud of me?"

"If you try again, yes," Sensei Wu replied. "If you quit . . . that he would not understand. Your father chose to be a different kind of hero, a kind I could never be. He knew he was the only one who could raise you and

Nya and keep you strong and safe. And, Kai, you are the only one who can do what needs to be done now."

Kai stood and walked back to his start position. Once again, he concentrated on the training dummy. He pictured every movement he would make, from his leap to sailing straight and true through the air toward the target. But this time, as he began to run, he felt something more than a determination to succeed. He knew he was running in the footsteps of his father.

I will learn everything Sensei Wu can teach me, Kai thought as he took off into the air. *I will rescue Nya, Father. I will carry on your legacy and make you proud.*

There was no confusion, no wasted motion now — simply a young man with **fire in his heart** doing what he must do. He was one with his body, and the world around him seemed to slow down. Then his left foot landed on the target dummy,

punching through the straw and sticks and rags. The dummy toppled as Kai landed cleanly on his feet.

Sensei Wu gave the barest of smiles. "Better. Today, you fought your first great enemy — your own doubts — and you won. Take that victory into your tomorrows and you will bring honor to your name . . . and to the memory of your father."

"Whew!" said Kai. "After all that, I'm thirsty. Got any more of that tea?"

Sensei Wu smiled. "Snatch the cup from my hand without disturbing the tea inside . . . and we'll talk."

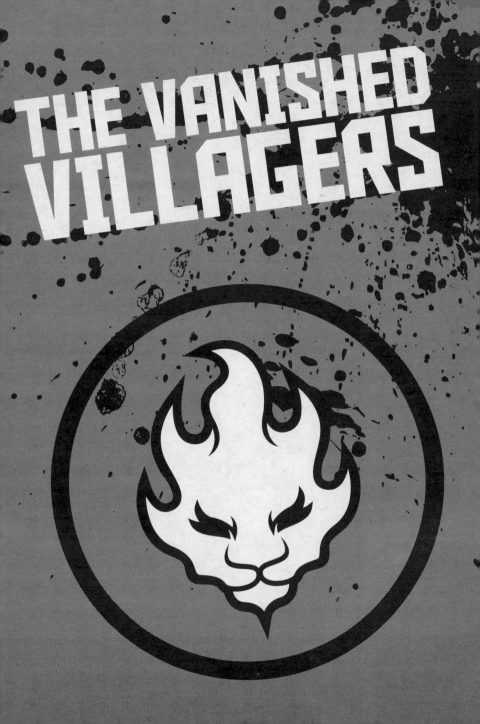

THE VANISHED VILLAGERS

CHAPTER 1

Kai raised his axe and brought it down in one smooth motion, splitting a log with a loud crack. He had been chopping firewood for over an hour now and already had far more than was needed.

At least this makes me feel like I am doing something, thought the young ninja. *All this waiting around is going to drive me crazy!*

He put another log in place. As he lifted the axe, he imagined the log was the skeleton warrior who had kidnapped his sister, Nya. Kai had joined Sensei Wu's team in order to rescue her, but so far they had been mainly

concerned with finding the Four Weapons of Spinjitzu. Kai knew that was important — the Weapons had awesome power, after all — but it didn't feel like the search was getting him any closer to Nya. When he thought of her as a prisoner of Samukai and the skeleton legion, it made him want to explode with rage.

Kai swung the axe a little too hard this time and turned the log into splinters. He was just brushing them off his red garment when he heard a voice behind him.

"You should take it easy. What did that log ever do to you?"

It was Zane, the Ninja of Ice, leaning against a tree with his arms folded across his chest. His tone of voice, as always, was serious. The saying around camp was that Zane wouldn't know a joke if it bit him.

If someone else had made that remark, Kai might have snapped at him. But he had learned to accept that Zane was different,

even if he didn't always understand his fellow ninja. Zane honestly didn't seem to get why other people reacted to things the way they did, particularly when it came to anger or other strong emotions.

"I was thinking of . . . other things," Kai replied.

"Oh," said Zane. "And these other things are upsetting you?"

"What was your first clue?" said Kai, turning back to his work.

"It was the way you were chopping down a half dozen trees for one night's campfire," Zane answered calmly. "You should save your energy, Kai, for the fights to come."

Kai threw down the axe and sat down on a stump. "**What fights?** All we do is chase around Ninjago looking for . . . things. Meanwhile, my sister is out there somewhere in terrible trouble, waiting for me to save her, and what I am doing? Camping out!"

There was a long silence. Then Zane said softly, "I envy you."

Kai looked over his shoulder. He couldn't believe he had heard that correctly. "Envy me? What's to envy? My sister is missing because I wasn't fast enough or tough enough to save her from the skeletons."

Zane flashed the barest hint of a smile. "You don't understand. I don't envy the fact that your sister is missing — it's that you *know* she is missing. You have memories of her. That is more than I have."

Kai rose and walked over to his friend. He had heard fragments of the tale of Zane's past, but never in detail. *I've been so caught up in my own problems, I never stopped to think about what his might be,* Kai said to himself.

"Did you have a sister?" asked Kai.

"That's just it. I don't know," said Zane. "Not so very long ago, I woke up on a road outside of a small village. I had no memory of where I was or how I had gotten there. The people of the village took me in and gave me a home, but they couldn't tell me who I was. All I did remember was my name.

"I lived there until Sensei Wu came to me and offered me a place on this team. I thought that by **adventuring** I might uncover some clues to my past. So far, though, there hasn't been time to investigate."

Kai frowned. The sensei had often told him that worrying about his sister might distract him at some crucial moment. Yet he allowed Zane to go on missions when the ninja's entire past was a blank. Wouldn't that be at least a little distracting?

"How far away is that village?" asked Kai.

"Five or six miles, I would guess," answered Zane. "Why?"

"Because we are going to pay the place a visit," Kai replied. "Sensei Wu says we won't be moving on for a day or so anyway. That gives us time enough to check the place

out and see if we can find answers to some of your questions. Let's go."

As the two ninja headed back to camp to get their gear, neither noticed a shadow detach itself from the larger darkness. It belonged to a skeleton warrior, who was even now rushing back to the Underworld with most interesting news.

CHAPTER 2

amukai, leader of the skeleton legions, steepled his bony fingers and smiled. "Fascinating. It is a shame you missed the first part of the conversation, Kruncha, but what you did hear might prove useful."

Kruncha bowed his skull and tried hard to contain his excitement. Samukai was pleased! This might mean a promotion, or even permanent assignment to the world of Ninjago.

"If Kai and Zane are going to this village, then there must be something of importance there," Samukai continued. "They would not

take time from their mission for anything less than a critical quest. That means we must get there first."

Kruncha, eyes still on the ground, said, "But, wise and powerful Samukai, what if the two ninja arrive while we are searching for . . . whatever is there? The treasure might be destroyed in the battle . . . along with the two ninja, of course," he added hurriedly.

Samukai rose from his throne. "That is why we will distract the two would-be heroes, giving us all the time we need to find what they are seeking. Assemble a squad. Here is what we will do . . ."

🔥 🔥 🔥

Kai and Zane moved quickly through the woods. The ice on the tree limbs glittered like gems in the sunlight. The snow on the ground was topped with a thick coating of frost, which crunched loudly beneath Kai's feet. The fire ninja envied how Zane

could move over the snow so lightly that he **left no trace**.

"You'll have to teach me to do that," Kai said.

Zane shrugged. "I'm not sure I can."

"Didn't Sensei Wu teach it to you?"

"No," Zane answered. "I've always known how to do this. Or, at least, I woke up that day knowing how."

"And there wasn't anything on you that might have hinted at where you came from?" asked Kai. "No mud stains, pieces of plant, anything that could have shown where you were before?"

Zane shook his head. "I don't think so. But at the time, I was so confused that I really didn't pay much attention."

"You're not going to make this detective thing easy, I can see," Kai said, smiling.

Zane stopped and pointed up ahead. "Well, I think that's what you would call a clue."

Through the trees, Kai could see a small village. Smoke curled from a dozen chimneys and the air was filled with the sounds of men and women working and children playing. It reminded him of his own home. Somehow, that made him even more determined to help Zane.

The two ninja swiftly reached the outskirts of the village. Zane immediately saw someone he knew, a large, balding tinkerer named Genn.

"Hello!" said Zane. "It is good to see you again."

"Zane?" Genn said, glancing around, as if afraid someone might have heard him. Kai didn't know the man, but his behavior made the young ninja a little uneasy.

"What . . . um, what brings you here?" asked Genn.

"I just wanted to see my home again," said Zane. "This is my friend Kai."

Genn nodded in Kai's direction, but

his eyes never left Zane. There was fear in those eyes. "You picked a very bad time to come," the tinkerer said, a little too quickly. "You know how, ah, busy we are at this time of year. Maybe . . . maybe you would prefer visiting some other day."

"Is something the matter?" asked Zane.

Kai already knew what the man's answer would be, and that it would be a lie.

"No, of course not," said Genn. "Just . . . just a busy time, that's all."

"Then my friend and I can help and the work will go faster," Zane replied.

Kai and Zane walked into the village. Everywhere they went, they were met with looks of fear, anger, even despair. It didn't take a genius to see that something was very wrong. But whenever they asked, they were told everything was just fine.

Zane took Kai on a quick tour — the road on which he was found, the hut in which he had lived, and the icy lake he had been

meditating in on the day he met Sensei Wu. At first glance, Kai saw no clues to the mystery of Zane's past, but he had to admit he wasn't looking very hard. He was too distracted by the reactions of the villagers.

"Are they usually so disturbed around here?" asked Kai.

Zane leaned against a tree and folded his arms across his chest. "I have to admit, I have seen happier faces at funerals," he said.

"Yeah, well, let's make sure it's not our funeral that's being planned," said Kai. "From now on, **keep your eyes open**. Somebody's in real trouble here, and it might be us."

The two ninja spent the rest of the day chopping wood and doing other chores around the village. When they were done, they were ushered to the nicest hut in the village. Kai stood at the window of his room, watching the sunset, lost in thought. He wondered how Zane must feel being back here, where everything was familiar and unfamiliar at the same time.

That night, the villagers held a feast for the heroes, or what passed for a feast in a place with little in the way of wealth or resources. Still, the people shared what little they had. Throughout the meal, no one seemed willing to look at either Kai or Zane in the eye. The conversation was strained and spoken in low tones. After a few hours, Kai began to feel very tired. He excused himself, went back to the hut, and fell sound asleep.

CHAPTER 3

He awoke the next morning. The bright rays of dawn were streaming in his window. Kai stumbled out of bed, wondering why it was so quiet. Normally, in a village like this, people were up and working hard before sunrise. *Then again, this seems to be a pretty odd town,* he reminded himself.

Zane was just waking up. "I guess I am out of practice at doing anything but ninja training," he said. "About an hour after you left the dinner, I started to feel really tired. I came back here and fell right into bed."

"Must have been all that exciting

conversation at the party," Kai said. "And I guess it knocked everyone else out, too, because I don't hear anyone working."

Zane got out of bed, a look of concern on his face. "You're right, neither do I. But that makes no sense. Genn's right, this is the busiest time of the year for the village. Feast or no feast, they wouldn't sleep in."

He went out the door, Kai following. The two stood in the village square, looking around. There was no one around — nobody working, no children at play, not even a dog lying in the morning sun. Zane went straight to Genn's hut and knocked on the door. There was no answer.

Pushing the door open, Zane went inside. Breakfast was set on the table, tea and a hunk of bread. A fire was dying in the hearth. There was **no sign of anyone**. The two ninja searched the place and the surrounding area, but saw no sign of Genn or his family.

It was the same at every other house in the village. There was evidence of people having been in the homes just recently, but they were gone now. It seemed as if they had simply all disappeared at the same moment.

"I can't believe this," said Zane. "How could it have happened?"

"And why didn't it happen to us?" asked Kai.

"Maybe we should go get the sensei and Cole and Jay. What do you think?"

Kai shook his head. "I know how you feel, but it would take hours to get back to camp and then bring them back here. Sensei Wu might not even want to take time away from training for our mission to investigate. No, we need to solve this **ourselves**."

Zane sat down on a bench, his head in his hands. "Kai . . . did we cause this?"

"What do you mean?"

"The people . . . they looked so afraid. Did someone or something target them because we were here? Did we bring trouble to my home?"

Kai sat down next to him. "I don't know, Zane. But, whatever happened, we'll make it right. Whoever did this doesn't know what trouble is — but we're going to teach him."

CHAPTER 4

The first question the ninja had to try to answer, of course, was whether someone did something to the villagers or they did it to themselves. They had obviously been terrified of something, so the possibility existed that they had packed up and fled in the night.

"I could believe that, except for one thing," Zane said when Kai suggested the theory. "They didn't pack up. It doesn't look like anything's gone but the people."

"We're missing the easy answer," Kai replied. "Tracks — there's snow on the ground, so there have to be tracks showing where everyone went."

But there weren't any tracks. The two ninja searched the outskirts of the village, making a complete circle, and finding nothing beyond the marks left by squirrels and other small animals. In a number of places, there were faint lines in the snow, as if some kind of tool or machine had passed over. Whatever it had been, it hadn't been carrying people, as the lines weren't deep enough in the snow. Kai even tried climbing up on the roof of the tallest building, but all he could see in the distance was trees and snow. By the time he and Zane met up again, the Ninja of Fire was feeling extremely frustrated.

"This is impossible!" he snapped. "Even if they were taken, there would have to be some sign. They didn't just fly up into the sky and disappear."

"Maybe we're thinking about the wrong direction," Zane answered, pointing down

to the ground. "Remember, Sensei Wu told us there are openings to the Underworld in various places. Maybe this is one of them. The skeletons could have stolen them away through such a portal, which would explain why there are no tracks leading out of the village."

Kai's expression turned grim. "So Samukai took them the same way he took my sister. Zane, we have to find that portal and get them back."

Zane nodded. "Agreed. What does a portal to the Underworld look like?"

Kai started to answer, then stopped. He suddenly realized he had no idea what such a thing would look like. It was pretty doubtful there would be a sign nearby reading, "This Way to the Underworld." As stupid as some of the skeletons were, even *they* weren't that dumb.

"Well, um, we'll know it when we see it, I'm sure," he answered finally.

The two began a methodical search of the village, checking every house and every patch of snow-covered ground for any sign of an entry point. All the while, Zane was troubled. It wasn't just the mystery of what had happened to his friends and neighbors. He knew worrying too much about them would distract him from spotting the answer to the puzzle. No, it was those lines he and Kai had seen in the snow all around the village. Their pattern seemed familiar somehow.

It was now late afternoon. Zane had run out of places to search. He went to find Kai to share the disappointing news that he had found nothing. He discovered his friend in a shed behind one of the huts, banging around among the owner's tools. Now and then, a hammer or a shovel would come **flying out** of the door.

"It has to be here," Kai was muttering. "They must have it well hidden. It's probably

under that pile of tools under there. No, I looked there already. . . ."

Cautiously, in case more tools came flying out, Zane opened the door to the shed. He was about to call out to Kai when he saw something hanging on the wall. Of course! It was so simple! No wonder they hadn't found any tracks.

"A rake!" he exclaimed.

"What? *Ow!*" said Kai, turning to see his friend and banging his head on a shovel in the process.

"The lines in the snow, the ones we saw all over," said Zane. "They were the marks left by a rake."

"Who rakes snow? Shovel it, sure, but rake it?" said Kai.

"Think about it," Zane continued. "If you had left footprints in the snow and wanted to obliterate them, what would you do? Run a rake over them. There were traces, all right, but someone went to a lot of trouble to hide them."

Kai smiled. "All right, now we have some-thing. I'm not sure what, but it's something. Still, those marks were all over the outskirts. They don't tell us which direction the villag-ers went."

Zane hadn't thought of that. Still, it made sense. If they really wanted to keep things secret, it wouldn't make sense to only rake over one trail. That would stand out too much if it was spotted. It would be more effective to run the rakes all around the vil-lage so there would be no way to tell which concealed trail had been the right one.

"That's true," said the Ninja of Ice. "But perhaps—"

"**Quiet!**" Kai whispered. "I thought I heard something."

Now Zane heard it, too. Someone was sneaking around outside. They might have been making an effort to keep quiet, but the crunching snow was giving them away. He edged over toward the small window in

the rear of the shack. The glass was covered with a thick coating of frost, but Zane could just barely see that someone was moving around outside.

Zane signaled to Kai that he would try to distract the intruder while Kai slipped around the right side of the building to nab him. As soon as Kai snuck out the door, Zane said loudly, "No, Kai, I don't think we should just quit and go home. What? No, the people of this village don't play practical jokes. I really don't think—"

There were sounds of a scuffle coming from outside. Zane darted outside to see that Kai had transformed into a **fiery whirlwind** using the power of Spinjitzu, and was battering a skeleton warrior senseless with the snow and ice stirred up by his tornado. As Kai slowed down, Zane ran forward and grabbed the skeleton.

"What are you doing here?" Zane demanded. "Be warned, my friend here can do far worse than hurl snowballs at you."

The skeleton went from dazed to defiant in a matter of moments. "I won't tell you anything. I don't know anything."

"That I can believe," said Kai. "You guys aren't exactly hired for your brains . . . or your good looks, for that matter. Anyway, we don't need you to talk, we know what happened. You boneheads kidnapped the people of this village and now you want a ransom, right?"

The skeleton's face brightened. "Right . . . I mean, no. We didn't take the villagers. They, um, fled because they knew we were coming."

"And why were you coming to a tiny village like this?" pressed Zane. "What's here that Samukai could be interested in?"

The skeleton's jaws clamped shut. He had evidently remembered he wasn't supposed to be talking.

"Hey, Zane, do you know what's left of bone after a fire?" asked Kai.

"No, what?" answered Zane.

Kai leaned in very close to the skeleton warrior. "Not a whole lot."

"Okay, okay!" said the skeleton. "It's . . . it's . . ." He dropped his voice to a whisper. "It's the treasure."

Kai and Zane looked at each other, then back at their prisoner, confused. "What treasure?" asked Zane.

"There's a legion on its way to get it," the skeleton hissed. "We know just where it is in the village."

"Then why don't you tell us, and we'll all know," said Kai. "Zane, do you know anything about a treasure hidden here?"

Zane shook his head. "No, but I would certainly like to hear more."

The skeleton warrior suddenly wrenched himself loose from the grasp of the ninja and started running toward the shed. Before Kai or Zane could stop him, he dove through the small window and into the building.

"Well, that was a silly thing to do," said Kai as the two ninja ran around to the front of the shed. "Does he think we won't be able to find him?"

Zane grabbed Kai and shoved him down to the ground. "I think he was counting on us finding him. Duck!"

A thrown axe **sliced the air** just above the ninja's heads. It was followed by shovels, rakes, and knives, all hurled through the open door of the shed by the skeleton warrior inside. The storm of tools kept the two ninja pinned down.

"He has to run out of ammunition eventually," said Kai.

"What if his aim gets better in the meantime?" Zane answered. "I have an idea."

The Ninja of Ice sprang to his feet, braced for battle. As the sharp tools flew at him, he batted them aside with eye-blurring speed. Then, somehow, he missed a strike. A hammer made it past his defenses and

struck him a glancing blow on the head. Zane hit the ground hard and lay still.

"Zane! Are you all right?" said Kai.

The Ninja of Ice opened one eye. **"Shhhh.** It just looked like the hammer hit me, but don't let our friend inside know that. Now you try."

Kai jumped up and ran for the shed. He made it halfway there before a thrown shovel brought him down, or seemed to. Like Zane, he lay still and quiet in the snow.

After a few minutes, the skeleton warrior peeked out the door of the shed. Seeing both his enemies were unconscious, he smiled. Samukai would certainly reward him for finishing off two such dangerous foes. He picked up a shovel and took a step toward where Kai was sprawled on the ground.

Then he stopped and thought. *Didn't Samukai say something about these ninja?* **What was it?** *Leave them a lamp? Leave them a loaf? No, no, that wasn't*

it. I know it was important. Leave them . . .
leave them . . .

Alive! That's it. Leave them alive!

He dropped the shovel. It landed on his foot, making him yell so loud he almost startled Kai into moving. Grumbling, the skeleton hobbled off to the east and was soon out of the village.

As soon as he was gone, Zane and Kai got to their feet. Keeping behind the cover of buildings, they watched as the skeleton limped toward the woods.

"Once he is inside the forest, we will trail him," said Zane. "I still think the skeletons captured my friends for some reason and he will lead us right to them."

"So you don't think there's a treasure here?" asked Kai.

Zane gestured toward the simple huts all around. "Does it *look* like there's a treasure here?"

"Hey, my blacksmith shop just looked like

a blacksmith shop," Kai replied. "How was I to know a map to the Four Weapons of Spinjitzu was hidden there? You never know what someone might think is a good hiding place."

Zane wasn't paying attention. His eyes were on the skeleton warrior, who was now about fifty yards from the edge of the woods. Then, to the ninja's amazement, the skeleton simply disappeared.

The two ninja raced to the spot where the warrior had last been seen. The skeleton's footprints in the snow abruptly stopped, but there was nowhere nearby he could be hiding. He was just gone.

"Come on, we'll search the woods," Kai said. "He must be here somewhere."

"The sun's setting," Zane answered. "It will be pitch-dark in a few minutes. We won't spot him and we might be walking into an ambush. Better to wait for morning."

"The sun's setting," Kai repeated. "The sun's . . . **Wait a minute!** Something isn't right here!"

Kai ran back into the village, straight to the house he and Zane were sharing. He ran to his window and stared out at the darkness. "I can't see it. That explains everything."

"Can't see what? I don't know what you're talking about," said Zane.

"The sunset," said Kai. "Last night, I saw the sun setting outside this window. But this morning, I saw the sun *rising* outside this same window."

"That's impossible," said Zane. "That would mean the window was facing west at night —"

"— and east in the morning," Kai finished for him. "A lot of 'impossible' things have been happening around here, and I think now I know why."

Zane frowned. "So it's not the same window?"

"You're thinking too small," said Kai,

smiling. "It's not the same house. It's not the same village. We've been tricked, Zane. The only thing I'm not sure of is why."

The two ninja stayed up all night, keeping watch for an attack by the skeletons. None came. In the morning, Kai led Zane back to the spot where they had seen the skeleton disappear.

"They couldn't afford to move us too far from where we had been before, or we might have noticed that the stars were all different," the Ninja of Fire explained. "But they had to make sure we couldn't see the answer. **Stand back.**"

Kai picked up a rock and threw it with all his might toward the woods. Fifty yards short of the line of trees, it struck something and dropped to the ground. Zane's eyes widened as a spiderweb of cracks suddenly appeared in empty space. He went to the spot where the rock had impacted and reached out. Where he would have expected to feel nothing but cold air, he instead felt a smooth, hard surface.

"It's a mirror," said Kai, "a big one, too. There are probably others around as well. Makes it look like there's just trees and snow all over. Our pal didn't vanish—he just slipped behind the mirror."

"Then that is where we're going, too," said Zane.

CHAPTER

Samukai smacked the skeleton warrior who stood before him with two of his four hands. Then he smacked him with the other two for good measure.

"Idiot," the ruler of the Underworld growled. "Dumb pile of bones. I gave you a simple job, and you screwed it up."

"But, Master, I defeated them in battle and successfully escaped," the skeleton whined. "I thought you would be pleased."

Samukai sat down hard on his throne of bones. "Understand something: The day I want Kai and Zane defeated, it will happen without aid from you. The point of this exercise was not a test of strengths, but a masterpiece of deception."

It had, truly, been one of Samukai's most inspired ideas. He knew two of Sensei Wu's ninja would not be visiting a tiny village just for fun. There had to be some treasure concealed there that Wu wanted to get his hands on. He could have simply had skeletons keep an eye on Kai and Zane and pounce when they grabbed the treasure, but what if one of the villagers took it and hid it in the meantime? No, he had to know the precise location of the ninja's goal and then be able to get it without their interference.

And so he put his plan into action. First, Kruncha and a large group of skeleton warriors **descended** on the village. While a few remained behind to make sure the villagers behaved, the rest went to work building a duplicate of the village not far away. Giant mirrors would keep the ninja from spotting any signs of the real village when they were in the fake one.

Unfortunately, Kruncha's bumblers were not yet done when Kai and Zane arrived. At Kruncha's direction, the villagers made the ninja welcome, or as welcome as frightened humans could. That night, during the feast, they gave the two ninja tea with certain herbs in it that put them to sleep. The skeletons then transported Kai and Zane to the fake village.

The plan was simple. The ninja would wake up and be faced with the mystery of the disappearing villagers. Fearful, they would race to retrieve the treasure, not knowing they were being spied upon by the skeletons. Once the hiding place was revealed, Samukai would be notified and his warriors would get the treasure from its place of concealment in the real village.

The ninja surprised the skeletons. They did not go searching for the treasure, but the villagers. Impatient, Samukai sent a warrior in

with instructions to get captured and further motivate the ninja to get the treasure. That had not worked out well.

"They will be on their way there," muttered Samukai, "in search of the treasure. And as soon as they have it . . . we will take it away from them."

CHAPTER 6

When Kai and Zane slipped around behind the giant mirror, they should not have been surprised by the sight that greeted their eyes . . . yet, still, they were. There, not far in the distance, was Zane's village. It had been so close all the time and they had never been aware of it.

"Let's go," said a determined Zane. "Someone is going to pay for tricking us."

"Not so fast," said Kai. "Look."

On the outskirts of the village, skeleton warriors were patrolling in pairs. Beyond them, villagers could be seen working under the watchful eye sockets of more skeletons. The little town was now an armed camp.

"I see," said Zane. "If we go charging in there, innocents might get hurt. But we can't just leave them all to be prisoners of the skeletons."

"What does Sensei Wu always tell us? 'Use your opponent's strength against him,'" answered Kai. "Well, what do the skeletons want? Based on what our ex-captive said, they think there's treasure in the village. They probably also think we know where it is. So let's **lead them to it**."

Zane looked at his friend, puzzled. "How? There is no treasure."

Kai smiled. "But they don't know that. Come on, we have a lot of work to do."

By that evening, the two ninja were ready. Carrying shovels, they slipped into the woods close to the edge of the real village. They crouched down by a pair of tree stumps

and watched the skeletal guards on patrol for a few moments. Then Kai whispered, "Stay here."

The Ninja of Fire got to his feet and moved off, purposely letting the moonlight reveal him to the skeletons. The two warriors immediately started following Kai into the woods.

My friend was right, thought Zane. *They didn't attack him. They want to know where he's going and what he might find there.*

Once Kai was sure he was being followed, he started walking faster. Then he began to run. Behind him, the skeletons were running, too. They knew that losing sight of the ninja now would mean punishment from Samukai.

Kai spotted the old, rotted log he and Zane had left as a marker. He picked up speed and **leaped**, landing in the snow about ten feet past the log. He turned to see the pair of skeletons jumping over the log. There was a series of sharp cracks and the two warriors disappeared from view, falling into the concealed pit Kai and Zane had dug. Some sticks and some snow had hidden it well until it was too late.

"That's two down," said Kai.

Not far away, Zane had his own trap set. Once he was certain he had attracted skeleton attention, he went to work. Scurrying halfway up a hillside, he came to a natural rock wall. He immediately started banging one of the large rocks with his shovel, attempting to wrestle it free, and muttering angrily about how stubborn the stupid piece of stone was turning out to be. Finally, he threw up his hands in seeming frustration and stalked off.

Once he was well clear of the spot, Zane hid to watch what would happen. After a few minutes, a pair of skeletons raced over to the wall and wrenched the rock free. They had about two seconds to feel proud of their accomplishment before the entire wall

collapsed on them, followed by the ton of snow the wall had been holding back.

Satisfied they would be digging themselves out for the rest of the night, Zane moved on to his next targets.

🔥 🔥 🔥

For the next three hours, Kai and Zane whittled down the numbers of the skeleton warriors. Now it was getting tricky. Samukai, Kruncha, and three skeletons were in the town meeting hall, along with all the villagers. Two other skeletons were in the center of town, mounted on a Turbo Shredder vehicle. The fearsome machine, with its skull grill and chomping, front-mounted "jaws," could end the ninja's night in a big hurry.

"I know how to get the villagers free," said Zane. "But we need the Shredder to do it. Any ideas?"

Kai smiled. "Let's head for the toolshed. I think it's time to chop some wood."

Later, Zane sat high in a tree, ready to

spring their trap. Down on the ground, Kai was calculating distance. "Okay, when I pass Genn's house, you need to start cutting," the Ninja of Fire said. "The timing has to be just right, or else Sensei Wu is going to be short two ninja."

"Good luck," said Zane.

Kai waved and ran off into the village. He raced right up to the Turbo Shredder and started jumping up and down, saying, "You guys couldn't catch a cold! The other ninja wanted to help, but I told them I could handle twenty skeletons by myself. What did you think, that you snuck into this village without us noticing? We could hear your **bones rattling** a hundred miles away!"

The skeleton driver gunned the Turbo Shredder to life. Kai wheeled and ran for the woods, the vehicle on his heels. He could hear the jaws clamping down behind him and knew that if he so much as stumbled, he

wouldn't be getting up again. He sped past Genn's house, hoping that Zane saw him and was sawing away.

The Ninja of Ice had indeed spotted his friend. Counting down to himself, he sliced the thick ropes he and Kai had rigged up. He had just finished when Kai ran past, followed closely by the Turbo Shredder. The last strand of rope gave way then and the huge tree trunk the two ninja had rigged swung free.

The skeletons never knew what hit them. The tree trunk slammed into the Turbo Shredder, sending it rolling onto its side and hurling the two warriors out into the snow. Kai knocked them out with two well-placed chops as Zane scrambled down the tree.

"Help me get this thing back on its treads," said Kai. "Then we'll go pay a call on Samukai."

CHAPTER 7

Kai stood in front of the town hall. Light blazed within the building and he could hear the soft cries of children coming from inside. He wanted to march right in and pound Samukai and his skeletons for scaring all these innocent people, but better to stick to the plan. The important thing was getting Genn and the others out safe.

"Hey, skullface!" he shouted at the closed doors. "I have something you want!"

The door opened a crack. Kruncha poked his skull out. "Uh, like what?"

Kai shook his head. "I only talk to your

boss. Let's see his ugly face." When Kruncha hesitated, Kai added, "Or I could just take the treasure back to Sensei Wu like I'm supposed to."

Kruncha withdrew. An instant later, the door opened wider. Samukai, all four arms and fierce expression, appeared. He took a moment to size Kai up, and then said, "Where is it? And what is it?"

"Where you won't find it," answered Kai. "And you'll find out what it is when you get it, which you will . . . in exchange for the villagers."

"Sensei Wu is getting soft in his old age." Samukai chuckled. "Trading a treasure for a few dozen humans? And not even human warriors?"

"Some of us think all humans are important," Kai replied. "We're funny that way. Do we have a deal?"

"First, show me the treasure."

"No," said Kai. "First, show me the villagers.

I want to be sure you haven't . . . lost any."

"Fair enough." Samukai nodded. He barked an order to someone behind him. Then he flung the doors open wide. The villagers were all crowded in behind him, just where Kai wanted them.

"Now!" shouted the Ninja of Fire.

There was a roar like an angry dragon and then Zane smashed the Turbo Shredder through the back wall of the town hall. Skeleton warriors were scattered like leaves in a windstorm. The villagers surged forward, pushing Samukai ahead of them.

"Go! Run!" yelled Kai. "Get as far from here as you can!"

Inside the building, Zane was turning the Turbo Shredder this way and that, chewing up floor and furniture as the skeletons fled in terror. Two jumped out the windows while the third scrambled into the chimney and tried to climb up toward the roof (only to get stuck halfway).

Samukai got to his feet and brushed the snow off himself with his four hands. He glanced at the chaos inside the town hall, then at the fleeing villagers, and finally at Kai. "No treasure?"

"Guess not," said Kai.

"Then why did you and your friend come here?"

"I don't think you would understand," said Kai. "It's a human thing."

Samukai shrugged. "Probably not. You realize I could destroy you and your friend?"

Kai slipped into **battle-ready stance**. "I realize you could try."

The ruler of the Underworld smiled. It was a ghastly sight. "But if there is no treasure, there would be no point. We will meet each other again, little ninja, and all questions will be answered. For now, I see no need to soil my hands in combat with you. Oh, and you might tell your friend to turn off the engine. I am sure these people would like a town hall to return to, for the little time that is left to them."

Before Kai could respond, Samukai had vanished. *Evidently, I was right about one thing,* the ninja thought. *There is a portal to the Underworld in this town.*

CHAPTER

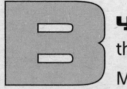y the next morning, the villagers had returned. Most looked ashamed for the part they had played in tricking the ninja.

"We had no choice," said Genn. "But that doesn't make it any better."

"It turned out all right," Zane assured him. "Kai and I have to move on, but I will be back to check on all of you. I don't think the skeletons will come back again. If they do, Kai and I will give them a proper welcome."

Genn gave Zane a hug. The other villagers came up to shake the ninja's hands, pat them on the back, and thank them for their

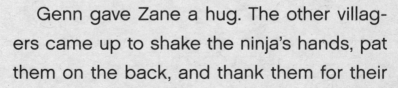

help. When everyone had had their say, Kai and Zane turned and left the village.

"Imagine those stupid skeletons," Kai said, laughing, "thinking there was some great treasure hidden there."

"Well, there was," Zane replied. "But they never would have recognized it."

"What do you mean?"

Zane looked back at the village. "Each and every one of those villagers welcomed me — a stranger — into their community. They gave me shelter and food and friendship. When I left, I did so knowing that if I ever needed to come back, they would take me in. That makes them the closest thing I have to family in this world."

Kai thought about his sister. She was all the family he had left in the world, and there was nothing he would not do for her. **"I get it,"** he said, "and you're right, Zane — that is a treasure."

The two walked on in silence for a while

before Kai said, "Hey. We got so wrapped up in solving the mystery in the village that we never learned anything about your past."

"I know," said Zane. "I still want to . . . need to . . . learn where I came from. But maybe for today, it is enough to think about where I am and with whom. Whoever I was before, it led me to good friends and a life with purpose. For the moment, I don't need more than that."

"Then let's get back," said Kai. "Maybe if we tell our tale well enough, Sensei Wu will forget to punish us for being gone so long."

"You don't really believe that," said Zane.

Kai did his best to look very serious. Then his expression cracked and he burst out laughing. "No, no, I really don't. We are so in for it, but **at least we got a good story out of all this**."